# SHOWS

Melissa was standing in the middle of the stage, and Todd was a little bit behind her. Sweeping music started pouring from the sound system. Melissa looked up toward the ceiling and opened her mouth to sing. Suddenly, a frog fell right on her face!

"AHHHHH!" she screamed. The frog ribbited loudly and hopped off her head and onto the ground. The whole audience began to laugh, thinking this was part of their act. But then another frog fell from the sky and landed in the audience. Then another and another and another!

**THE HARDY BOYS® SECRET FILES**

# THE HARDY BOYS®

## SECRET FILES #4

 Hopping Mad

BY **FRANKLIN W. DIXON**

ILLUSTRATED BY **SCOTT BURROUGHS**

ALADDIN • NEW YORK LONDON TORONTO SYDNEY NEW DELHI

ALADDIN

An imprint of Simon & Schuster Children's Publishing Division
1230 Avenue of the Americas, New York, NY 10020
This Aladdin paperback edition July 2022
Text copyright © 2010 by Simon & Schuster, Inc.
Illustrations copyright © 2010 by Scott Burroughs
All rights reserved, including the right of reproduction in whole or in part in any form.
ALADDIN is a trademark of Simon & Schuster, Inc., and related logo is a registered trademark of Simon & Schuster, Inc.
THE HARDY BOYS is a registered trademark of Simon & Schuster, Inc.
For information about special discounts for bulk purchases, please contact
Simon & Schuster Special Sales at 1-866-506-1949 or business@simonandschuster.com.
The Simon & Schuster Speakers Bureau can bring authors to your live event.
For more information or to book an event contact the Simon & Schuster Speakers Bureau
at 1-866-248-3049 or visit our website at www.simonspeakers.com.
Designed by Lisa Vega
The text of this book was set in Garamond.
Manufactured in the United States of America 0722 COM
10 9 8 7 6 5 4
Library of Congress Control Number 2010929646
ISBN 978-1-6659-3083-3 (prop)
ISBN 978-1-4424-0943-9 (eBook)

# CONTENTS

# Prepare to Die

Frank and Joe Hardy stood facing each other on an empty cliffside. Beneath them the ocean crashed and roared. In their hands each brother held a sharp metal sword. For a long minute they stared at each other. Suddenly, Joe screamed.

"AHHHHHHH!"

He came running at Frank, sword held high in the air! At the last moment, right as Joe swung his sword at his brother's head, Frank dove to the ground. He did a perfect front roll and rose to his feet gracefully, out of Joe's reach. Joe's sword hit only air, and he stumbled. Frank took advantage of Joe's momentary loss of balance and swung a vicious cut right at Joe's stomach. Joe managed to get his sword up, just barely in time to block his brother's blow.

They battled back and forth across the cliff. The only sound was the huffing and puffing of their breath, and the loud clash of metal on metal. Sometimes Joe seemed to have forced Frank into a corner, but at the last minute Frank would execute a daring escape. Other times Joe seemed almost at the

point of surrendering, only to come back with a powerful slice at Frank. Finally, after a round of cuts so fast the eye could barely follow, Joe had Frank disarmed and pressed up against the cliffside! His sword was at Frank's throat. He looked his brother in the eye and said, "My name is Inigo Montoya. You killed my father. Prepare to—"

"Boys! What are you doing? And are those my curtain rods?!"

Suddenly, the cliffside and roaring ocean disappeared, and Frank and Joe were standing in their backyard. In their hands they held metal curtain rods instead of swords. Their mother and Aunt Gertrude were leaning out the window of the kitchen. They didn't look happy. Joe lowered his curtain rod.

"Mom!" Joe yelled back. "We're getting ready for the school talent show, remember?"

"We're acting out the big sword fight scene from *The Princess Bride*," said Frank. *The Princess Bride* was

Joe and Frank's favorite movie. They'd each seen it seventeen times. The big fight between Inigo and Wesley was their favorite part. They'd probably watched just that scene more than a hundred times. They were sure it would be a big hit at the Bayport Elementary School's annual spring talent show.

Aunt Gertrude and their mother had now come out onto the lawn. The boys could tell that they were not happy: They had their hands on their hips and their eyes were narrowed.

"I don't know if it's safe for you boys to be hitting each other with those," said their mom. "One of you could lose an eye!"

"Yes," agreed Aunt Gertrude. "Those curtain rods could hurt somebody!" Aunt Gertrude had just moved in with them a few weeks earlier, and while it was usually great to have her around, sometimes it meant twice as many rules.

"But, Mom!" said Joe. "We need to practice.

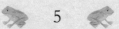 5

There's going to be a lot of competition." They'd been working on their routine for weeks! If they had to stop now, they would never have time to come up with something new.

"Yeah," chimed in Frank. "Cissy is going to be juggling four baseballs at the same time. And Melissa and Todd are going to be singing a duet!" Cissy "Speedy" Zermeño had the fastest hands on the local Little League team, the Bayport Bandits. She was good friends with Frank and Joe—but they still wanted to beat her in the talent show! And Melissa and Todd were like Bayport royalty— they'd once starred in a Tasty, Tasty Treats Ice Cream commercial, and they'd had the leads in every school play since kindergarten!

But Mrs. Hardy was not convinced.

"You can practice just as well with something less dangerous. Give me those."

She held out her hands. Frank and Joe shuffled

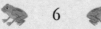

6

forward and sadly placed the curtain rods in her hand. All that practicing for nothing! They were out of the competition before it had even begun.

"Wait one second, boys." A smile grew on Aunt Gertrude's face. "I have an idea."

She ran back inside the house. The boys heard the sound of footsteps rushing up the stairs, and then the sound of the attic door slamming. A few minutes later Aunt Gertrude reappeared in the backyard.

"Here," she said happily. "You can use these." She held out two cardboard

tubes, the kind that wrapping paper came curled around. "I saw them when I was cleaning out the attic the other day. I was going to throw them out, but thankfully I forgot."

Frank and Joe each picked up a tube. They took a few practice swings. The tubes were just the right length! And they wouldn't hurt as much when they accidentally got hit. This was perfect!

"Thanks, Aunt Gertrude," the boys said together. Then Frank turned to face Joe. The backyard, Aunt Gertrude, and their mom disappeared from view. They were back on the rocky cliffside.

"En garde!" screamed Frank.

The battle was back on!

# Frogs Away!

**F**inally, two days later, the day of the talent show arrived! The boys had spent every spare moment practicing with the cardboard tubes that their aunt Gertrude had given them. They didn't make the same clashing sound that the metal curtain rods had made, but with a little bit of silver spray paint, they looked right. Their father even helped them build hilts on the base, so they looked like real swords.

9

The whole school was gathered in the auditorium to watch the talent show. Class had been canceled for the entire day! It didn't get any better. Everyone participating in the talent show drew numbers backstage to determine who went first. Frank drew number seven.

"I'm glad we're not first," said Joe.

"Scared?" said Frank.

"No!" said Joe. "I just don't want to intimidate the competition." And maybe he had a little stage fright. But just a little.

The first person up was Adam Ackerman. Frank and Joe watched from backstage.

"Ugh," said Joe. Adam was one of the school bullies, and he and the Hardys had never gotten along. He always had to be first at everything. Joe wouldn't have been surprised if he'd found a way to rig the drawing! All the other students in the talent show, along with Principal Butler, were waiting offstage and behind the curtain. Adam walked out onstage.

"What's big and gray and has sixteen wheels?" Adam asked. He paused to let the audience think.

"A truck!" someone yelled.

"Nope," said Adam. "An elephant on roller skates!"

As much as Frank hated to admit it, Adam's comedy routine was actually pretty funny. There was a reason he was one of the class clowns, after all. The audience was loving it. It seemed like they were going to have some stiff competition.

"What is green and smelly? The Hulk's farts."

Uh-oh. Principal Butler didn't look happy about that joke. She was frowning and her face was turning red! But the audience was hooting and laughing.

"What's brown and sticky?" said Adam. The audience grew quiet. It seemed like Adam was getting into dangerous territory with his jokes.

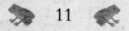

"A stick!"

By the time Adam was finished with his third joke, Principal Butler was already running out onto the stage. She grabbed him by the collar and took the microphone away from him.

"That's enough of that kind of talk, Mr. Ackerman," she said. "You are disqualified from this competition."

Some of the kids in the audience booed, but Adam just grinned. He waited until Principal Butler's back was turned, and then stuck out his tongue at her. The audience laughed again. Principal Butler whirled around, but by the time she looked at him, Adam was walking off the stage with his head down. He seemed pretty happy to have been pulled off the stage. Joe would have bet his favorite baseball mitt that that had been Adam's goal from the very beginning.

Next up, three girls from the fifth grade did a dance routine to a Madonna song. It was pretty good, but the audience didn't love it as much as they had loved Adam's jokes. After them a boy played the violin. It was beautiful—but not the sort of thing that won a talent show. Frank and Joe were feeling pretty good about their odds of winning . . . and pretty nervous!

Behind him, Frank heard a strange noise. He

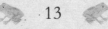

turned around and saw Mina, Adam's sister, crying on Principal Butler's shoulder.

"I can't do it!" she said. "I'm too scared."

"It's okay," said Principal Butler. "You don't have to go on if you don't want to."

It seemed like she had a bad case of stage fright! Frank understood how she felt. Still, he wasn't going to give up yet. Principal Butler got Mina to stop crying and sent her back into the audience. That made one less performance.

Now it was Cissy's turn. She walked onstage wearing her Bayport Bandits hat and clutching a baseball in each hand. Her hands were so small, the baseballs barely fit. She was the shortest student in their entire grade, but she made up for it by being twice as fast as anyone else. Whether she was running, talking, or pitching, she did everything double time. She began to juggle the two balls in one hand. The audience was not impressed.

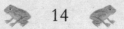

"I thought she was going to juggle four balls," Joe whispered to Frank.

"Me too," said Frank.

After a minute she looked over at Principal Butler and nodded her head. Principal Butler bent down and rolled a baseball toward her. Right as it got to her foot, Cissy kicked the ball like a Hacky Sack. It flipped up into the air—and she caught it! The audience cheered. Just like that, she went from juggling two balls to juggling three.

She juggled for a few minutes, sending the balls flying high and low. Sometimes she caught them under her legs or behind her back. She shifted the patterns they flew in. Each time she changed directions, the crowd cheered. She had them now!

Cissy switched to juggling all three balls with one hand. With her other, she reached up and pulled off her hat. Balanced on her head was the fourth baseball. She plucked it off her head and began to juggle all four!

"Yay, Cissy!" yelled Frank and Joe. They'd known she was good with a baseball, but they'd never known she was this good! She was going to give them a run for their money—but they wouldn't be sad if they lost to her. She deserved it.

Finally, Cissy caught all four balls in her hands and bowed. The crowd cheered. She walked off the stage. The boys grabbed her and congratulated her. She was smiling so wide, she couldn't even speak. It was the first time the boys had ever seen her speechless.

Now there was just one more act before Frank and Joe. They peeked out from behind the curtain. The school auditorium was packed! There must have been hundreds of people there. They had never before realized just how big their school was. . . .

"We should get ready," said Joe. Frank nodded.

But it wasn't until Melissa and Todd pushed past them that the boys were able to stop staring at the size of the audience.

"No competition here," Melissa said with a sniff as she walked onstage. Todd nodded.

They were wearing matching gold and black outfits. They looked kind of like taxicabs. They didn't seem impressed with any of the other acts. They always thought they were the best—and usually they were. They'd won the last two school-wide talent competitions.

They took their places. Melissa was standing in the middle of the stage, and Todd was a little bit behind her. Sweeping music started pouring from the sound system. Melissa looked up toward the ceiling and opened her mouth to sing. Suddenly, a frog fell right on her face!

"AHHHHH!" she screamed. The frog ribbited loudly and hopped off her head and onto the ground. The whole audience began to laugh, think-ing this was part of their act. But then another frog fell from the sky and landed in the audience. Then another and another and another!

Frank and Joe stared out from behind the curtain. The music was still blasting from the

stereo. The audience was panicking. Todd looked stunned, like someone had hit him with a shovel. Melissa was screaming. Principal Butler was trying to get her to calm down.

What was going on?

# 3

# Hoppin' Mad!

**F**rank and Joe ran out from the behind the curtain to grab the frogs that had fallen onto the stage. Luckily, they had years of experience at catching frogs, and it only took them a few minutes to get them all.

"Please be calm and stay seated!" Principal Butler had taken one of the microphones and was trying to get everyone to quiet down. Some of the students were chasing the frogs that had fallen among the seats. Others were running away from them!

Finally, after fifteen minutes, all the frogs were rounded up. A teacher walked through the audience with a big plastic bag, and everyone put the frogs they had captured inside. There was a fish tank in one of the third-grade classrooms, and the frogs would be put there until someone figured out where they came from.

Melissa and Todd were still standing on the stage. Melissa looked angry and

upset. Todd still looked shocked. But neither of them was going to leave until they'd had a chance to perform. Once everyone was seated, Melissa tried to wave to the sound people to get the music to start again. No one was paying attention to them. Instead, everyone was staring at Principal Butler, who was still holding the microphone. She didn't look happy.

"I am giving the person or people responsible for this prank exactly two hours to come forward or I will be forced to cancel the talent show entirely," she announced. Her face was so red it looked like a big tomato had been planted on her neck. Melissa and Todd gasped!

"Until that time, I am letting everyone out for an early recess. Anyone who has any information about this prank, please come talk to me in my office. You are dismissed."

Some of the students in the crowd cheered. But

 22

most of the students were upset. The annual talent show was a big deal at Bayport Elementary, and everyone wanted a chance to perform or watch their friends.

Melissa ran off the stage and pushed past Frank and Joe again. This time, she was crying.

"My big number!" she yelled. "Ruined! Why would someone do this to me?"

Frank and Joe looked at each other. They might not get a chance to show off their sword-fighting skills, but the Hardy Boys did have one other special talent—solving mysteries. And it looked like today was the day to show off that talent too.

"Who would want to ruin Melissa and Todd's big number?" said Joe.

"I don't know," said Frank. "Sure, they're a little annoying with their constant bragging, but they're both really good, and sweet, too—when they're not superbusy trying to win." Melissa and

Todd just got too competitive about things like this to remember that they were supposed to be fun. Maybe that attitude had rubbed someone the wrong way. Or maybe someone wanted to win the talent show this year and figured ruining Melissa and Todd's big number was the best way to do it. Either way, the boys had two hours to figure things out—before the talent show was canceled for good.

Frank pulled out his trusty notebook and pen.

The notebook was brown and battered from being carried in Frank's pocket all the time, but it had records of every crime they'd ever solved.

"All right, Joe. What do we know?"

# The Six *W*s of Crime Solving

**F**enton Hardy, Frank and Joe's dad, was a private investigator who used to work with the local Bayport police force. He'd been a cop in New York City for years. The boys had been watching him solve crimes since they were old enough to crawl after him. Over the years they'd learned more than a few things about figuring out unexplained events.

And the first was to start with the six *W*s of crime solving—What, When, Why, Who, How,

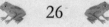

26

and Where. Frank and Joe found a quiet corner of the auditorium to sit down and think. Everyone else had gone out to recess, so they had the room to themselves.

Frank wrote down in his notebook: *What*.

"That part is easy," said Joe. "A rain of frogs!"

Frank wrote down *frogs* in the notebook. Then he kept going.

"What else are you writing?" asked Joe, curious.

Frank continued writing for a moment, then looked up and read from the notebook. "'Frogs. Falling from all around at the Bayport Elementary annual talent show. All specimens looked to be around the same age, size, species.'"

If there was one thing their father had specifically told them, it was that it paid to be as precise as possible. Solving a crime often rested on the details.

Frank wrote *When* next, under *What*.

 27

Joe looked at his watch. "It happened about twenty minutes after the talent show started, so around 11:20 a.m." Frank recorded the time in the notebook. After it he added *right at the beginning of Melissa & Todd's act*.

Joe scratched his head—a sure sign he was thinking about something.

"That means that the frogs must

have gotten into the auditorium earlier today. It couldn't have been last night, or they probably would have starved. And it couldn't have been that much earlier than the show itself, or they wouldn't have escaped at the right time."

"So whoever did this did it recently!" said Frank, excited. If the trail was still "warm," as their dad would say, they had a much better chance of catching the culprit.

"Okay," said Frank. "Next up is *Why*."

This one was tougher. In police investigations, this was known as the criminal's "motive." The boys took a few minutes to come up with as many reasons as they could as to why someone would want to drop frogs on the talent show.

"Someone hates frogs," said Joe.

"Someone hates Melissa and Todd," said Frank. He wrote both down. After that the list continued:

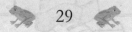 29

- Someone was out to ruin the talent show.
- Someone wanted to make Principal Butler angry.
- It was a prank directed at the school.
- It was an accident.
- They were a new species of frog that lived in the ceilings of public elementary schools. (Frank knew this was unlikely, but he'd always wanted to discover a new species of animal.)

"This isn't getting us anywhere," said Joe. Frank agreed. They had no way of knowing why someone would want to rain frogs down on the talent show. It was time to move on to the next piece of the puzzle: *Who*.

Who would want to sabotage the talent show?

"Well, Adam got pulled off the stage," said Frank. "And he's always starting fights and pulling pranks on people. Maybe he was angry at Principal Butler."

Adam was a pretty good suspect. They wrote his name down in the book. They thought for a few more seconds.

"Mina was freaked out about having to perform in front of the whole school," said Joe. "Maybe she did it so she wouldn't have to go on?"

"That's possible," said Frank. "But Mina is so nice. It doesn't seem like her. But like Dad says, you never know." Frank wrote Mina's name down too, even though they didn't think it could be her.

"I didn't see Adam or Mina when the frogs were falling, did you?" asked Joe.

Frank considered it for a second. He'd been pretty distracted. But now that he thought about it, he couldn't remember seeing either of them anywhere.

"So either one of them could be our prankster," said Joe.

"Or anyone else who wasn't at the show." Aside

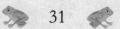

31

from Melissa, Todd, Cissy, and Principal Butler, it could have been almost anyone. The crowd was so big, no one would have noticed if one person was missing.

Carefully Frank wrote *Where* in the notebook. His hand was starting to get tired. He was glad that they'd be soon done with the writing part of the investigation.

"The first frog hit Melissa in the face," said Frank.

"But where did it come from?" said Joe.

"If someone was throwing them from the audience, they'd have to be pretty strong," said Frank. "And have good aim."

"Maybe they fell from the ceiling?"

Both boys looked up. How would frogs have gotten into the ceiling? Frank wrote it down, then crossed it out. That would be impossible.

"We've got two suspects," said Frank. "Should we start with them?"

Joe nodded. Frank flipped his notebook shut and the boys headed out to find Adam and Mina. First stop: the playground.

# 5

# A Confession!

Of the two, Adam seemed like the more likely suspect. It was hard to see Mina touching a frog, let alone throwing it at someone's face—no matter how scared she was to perform. Adam had a history of causing trouble. Frank and Joe had already run up against him once on a case, when they were trying to find the missing money from a video-game competition.

It wasn't hard to guess where Adam would be. If it was recess, he was over by the swings. That's where he and his friends—all the biggest and meanest kids in school—liked to hang out. They didn't even play on the swings. They just knew other kids wanted to use them, and liked standing next to them so everyone else would stay away.

The whole school was talking about the frogs. No one had any idea how it could have happened. As they walked across the school yard, Frank and Joe heard all different kinds of theories.

"I heard it was Principal Butler herself. She, like, went crazy or something. They took her away in a strait jacket!" That was Madison Tillery, the most popular girl in school. She had a whole circle of girls around her, listening wide eyed. They were all texting the story to friends at other schools while they listened to Madison.

"I'm tellin' you, it was aliens!" That was Chet Morton. He was a good friend of Frank and Joe's. He was talking loudly to a group of kindergartners.

 35

"I saw a whole TV show about it. They pick up frogs, and then they— Oh! Hey, Frank! Hey, Joe! Are you guys going to figure this mystery out?" Chet knew all about their cases, and had even been inside the tree house where they wrote them all up on a big chalkboard.

"We're going to try," said Frank.

"Nuh-uh," corrected Joe. "We're going to succeed!"

"Cool," said Chet. "Here's a lead for you: aliens!"

Frank laughed. Chet *always* thought it was aliens. Frank and Joe continued on their way. Finally, they made it over to the far side of the playground, where the swings were. Sure enough, there was Adam—along with Jeffrey Perkins, Susie Merrell, Joe Stracy, and Ian Williams. The five of them added together would have made ten of Frank or Joe. They towered above all the other kids in the third grade. Adam had his back turned as the boys approached, and was talking loudly to his friends.

"Did you hear me up there?" Adam was saying. "They loved me! If Principal Butler hadn't pulled me off the stage, I would have won the talent show, no questions. I was cheated!"

It sounded like Adam was pretty upset at Principal Butler. That would be reason enough to ruin the show. And if he thought he deserved to win on top of it . . .

"What do *you* want?" Susie asked. She had

noticed Frank and Joe, listening to Adam. She had a mean look in her eyes. She was probably the smartest of the third-grade bullies. All the other girls went running when she came into the cafeteria.

Joe swallowed loudly. "We, uh, we wanted to talk to Adam about the frogs." He was trying not to be afraid. Or to be afraid, but still do the right thing. That was what their dad had taught them.

"Did I say you could talk?" asked Susie. She pushed the other kids aside and walked up to Joe. She was a good two inches taller.

"Well, you did ask me—," Joe began.

"'Well, you did ask me. Nah, nah, nah,'" Susie copied him. Adam and the other kids laughed.

"Look, we just want to know if he had anything to do with the frogs that interrupted the talent show," said Frank.

"Goody Two-Shoes!" yelled Ian.

"You think I did that?" asked Adam. He walked over to Frank and Joe. The other kids came with him. Quickly, Frank and Joe were surrounded.

"It couldn't have been Adam!" A voice rang out from behind the circle of third-grade bullies. A second later, Mina wormed her way through the wall of kids.

"What do you mean, it couldn't have been Adam?" said Frank. He had pulled out his pen and notebook, eager to get another clue on the case. The bullies had already been forgotten.

"Hey, Mina, be quiet!" Adam looked nervous all of a sudden.

Mina ignored him. "He was with me!" she said.

Adam started waving his hands and trying to cut her off. "Don't listen to her!" he said. Now Frank and Joe were really curious. What was she going to say? All of Adam's friends were staring at Mina as well.

"He was—"

But Mina never got to finish her sentence. Adam

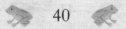

put his hand over her mouth. "Fine!" he said. "You caught me! I did it."

"What?" said Joe.

"I did it! I threw the frogs onstage. You can go tell Principal Butler. In fact, let's go do that right now."

Adam still hadn't removed his hand from Mina's mouth. She was staring at Frank and Joe, trying to get their attention. As Adam talked, she shook her head. It seemed like Mina didn't believe Adam. And neither did Frank or Joe. What was he trying to hide?

But it was too late to try and find out now. Adam was on his way to Principal Butler's office pushing Mina in front of him! Frank and Joe hurried to follow him. Could this be the end of the mystery after all?

# 6

## Guilty?

"Do you think Adam did it?" Frank asked Joe as they ran along behind him.

"No way!" said Joe. "But he is hiding something."

What could be so bad that he would rather get in trouble for something he didn't do? Only Mina knew—and Adam wouldn't let her tell!

By now, the word had spread throughout the school yard, and a crowd of kids were following Adam to Principal Butler's office.

"I guess it wasn't aliens," Chet said as he fell in step with Frank and Joe.

"Yeah," said Frank. "But I don't think it was Adam, either!"

Frank sped up. He managed to catch up with Adam right as they got to the door of the school.

"Adam!" he said. "You don't have to do this. Joe and I are going to find the person who really ruined the talent show."

Frank stood between Adam and the door. Since Adam was still holding Mina, he couldn't push Frank out of the way.

"Move!" he yelled. But Frank wouldn't budge.

"No way. Not until you tell the truth."

The other kids were beginning to whisper. Was Frank right? He and Joe had a reputation for finding out the truth. But why would Adam admit to something he hadn't done?

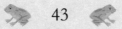

Adam took his hands off of Mina. It looked like he was going to shove Frank out of the way. But as soon as Mina was free, she started yelling again.

"He didn't do it!" Mina said. "He—"

But she didn't get any further before Adam had his hand over her mouth again. This time he bent down and whispered in her ear. After a minute Mina nodded. Adam let go of her mouth. This time, she didn't say anything.

Adam turned back to face Frank. He snapped his fingers and pointed. Ian and Susie each grabbed one of Frank's arms.

"Hey! Let me go!"

Ian and Susie carried Frank out of the way and dropped him down on the grass. Adam entered the school.

"You okay?" Joe asked Frank.

 44

"I'm fine. We've got to catch up with them!"

By the time Frank and Joe pushed through the crowd of kids around the school door, it was too

late. They just barely caught sight of Adam walking into the principal's office. They ran down the hall after him.

"Yes, Principal Butler," said Adam as Frank and Joe entered Principal Butler's office. "I did it. I threw the frogs at Melissa."

Principal Butler's mouth tightened into a hard line. She pushed her glasses back up the bridge of her nose.

"Well, Mr. Ackerman," she said. "I should have known."

Adam looked upset by that, but he didn't say anything.

"Where did the frogs come from?" Principal Butler asked.

"Uh . . . I . . . well... I caught them?"

"And how did you get them into the auditorium?"

"I smuggled them in under my coat."

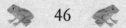 46

"He's not even wearing a coat!" yelled Frank.

"Shut up!" said Adam.

"He's lying!" said Joe.

Principal Butler paused, considering what the boys had said. It seemed pretty obvious that Adam wasn't telling the truth. She looked back and forth between Adam and the Hardy brothers. Then she shook her head.

"Adam has confessed. The talent show will continue. You, Mr. Ackerman, will be seeing me in detention this afternoon. And for the rest of the month. I'll let your parents know you'll be home late from now on."

Principal Butler picked up the phone and began to dial Adam's parents. Adam screwed his face up, like he couldn't decide whether to be happy or upset.

"That's not fair, Principal Butler!" said Joe. "He didn't do it."

Principal Butler ignored him and continued dialing the phone. After a few seconds the sound of Mrs. Ackerman's voice mail could be heard. Principal Butler hung up the phone. She checked her watch.

"I have a meeting right now. I need all of you to leave my office." She looked tired.

Frank opened his mouth to say something.

"I heard you before, Mr. Hardy. If you don't

think Adam did it, find out who did. He has confessed, and that's good enough for me. You have thirty minutes before my meeting ends and I call his parents again. Good-bye."

Principal Butler pointed to the door. Reluctantly, Frank and Joe left. Adam was right behind them.

"Not you, Mr. Ackerman. You can stay right here. Your detention starts now."

# 7

# Up, Up, and Away!

It looked like the entire school was waiting outside Principal Butler's office when Frank and Joe came out. Everyone wanted to be near the door when it opened.

"Did Adam do it? Is the talent show back on? Is he going to be expelled?"

A dozen voices asked the same questions as Frank and Joe walked away, but they just shook their heads. Adam had confessed . . . but they were sure he was innocent. Nothing was adding up.

  50

"What do we do now?" asked Joe after they had pushed their way clear of the crowd.

"I don't know," said Frank. "Thirty minutes isn't a lot of time to figure out this mystery." Frank looked up at the clock. It wasn't even thirty minutes anymore. Now it was more like twenty-eight minutes! Time was running out fast.

"What would Dad say?" asked Joe. He paused for a moment.

"Start with the evidence," the boys said at the same time.

"The frogs are gone," said Frank. "So the only evidence would be back in the auditorium itself. Maybe we missed something. Let's go look."

Joe didn't have a better idea, so the boys headed back to the school auditorium. From outside, they heard voices shouting.

"No! Stop that!"

What was happening? Could the prankster be

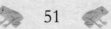

causing trouble again? Frank and Joe shoved open the doors and rushed inside.

On the stage, Melissa was chasing Todd around. She had taken off her yellow-and-black checkered cap, and was trying her best to hit him with it. But Todd had longer legs and was managing

to keep just outside her reach.

"You keep starting the second chorus too soon! You're cutting off my line." Melissa swung her hat again, and Todd skipped backward.

Out of the corner of her eyes, Melissa must have caught a glimpse of Frank and Joe. She spun around quickly.

She hid the hat behind her back, and a big fake grin lit up her face.

"Well, hello there!" She beamed. "Our performance has been put off for a little while, but we'll be on in just a bit! But it's always good to see our fans."

She gave a little bow. She seemed surprised to find Frank and Joe still standing there when she straightened up. The grin left her face.

"You can leave now," she said.

"Actually, we've got a few questions for you," said Frank. He took out his notebook and got ready to record her statement.

"Oh!" said Melissa. "You want an autograph. Of course."

Melissa hopped down off the stage and ran over to Frank. She grabbed the pen and notebook from his hand.

*To my biggest fan!* ❤ *Melissa.* She wrote in big curl-

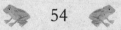

54

script, and she dotted her letter *i*'s with stars. But that wasn't the information Frank wanted.

"Thanks, but we wanted to ask you about the frogs. Did you notice anything strange before they started to appear?"

Melissa put one hand dramatically to her forehead. "I'm still too upset to talk to the press," she said. "I might faint."

She sat down dramatically on one of the chairs.

Frank shrugged.

"What about you?" Joe yelled out to Todd.

"Me?" Todd seemed surprised anyone would talk to him. Apparently, he was used to Melissa getting all the attention.

"Did you see anything strange?"

But before Todd could answer, Melissa was back on her feet.

"It was horrible! Simply horrible. There I was, ready for my big number, when that frog hit me

 55

smack in the face! It was cold and wet and awful. And I know Principal Butler thinks it was a prank on the talent show, but I know I was the target. Whoever did it must have read the interview I gave to the school newspaper, where I talked about my love of frogs and how I would never want to see them hurt. Did you read that issue? I have signed copies if you want one. When I'm famous—I mean, more famous than I am now—I'm going to start a charity for frogs."

Once Melissa started talking, there was no stopping her. Frank tried to jump in, but Melissa just kept going.

"It must be one of those crazy stalkers that celebrities get. I guess this is going to be my life from now on, so I had better get used to it. It's the price of fame."

Melissa paused to take a breath, and Frank jumped in.

"But where did the frogs come from? Did you see anything?" If they could figure out where the frogs had come from, maybe they could find some evidence of who brought them in the first place.

"What? I—I don't remember." Melissa was stumped.

"Did someone throw them from the audience? Or from backstage?"

Todd had been lingering in the background, listening to their conversation. Now he jumped in.

"They weren't thrown," he said. "I saw the one that hit Melissa fall from a crack in the ceiling—right up there."

Todd pointed above their heads. Frank and Joe peered up at the ceiling. It was too dark to make out much of anything all the way up there. It must have been thirty feet above their heads! But if that was where the frogs came from, that was where they had to go. Now, how could they get up there?

 57

# 8

# The Case Takes
a Turn . . .

**F**rank and Joe split up and searched around the auditorium for a way to get to the ceiling. For a few minutes neither of them said anything. Then Joe yelled out. "Over here!" He'd found something.

There were no stairs leading up, but at the back of the stage, behind the curtain, there was a tall metal structure, like a jungle gym. It was used to hang the lights for the plays. It went all the way up to the ceiling. It wouldn't be an easy climb. The

 59

bars were spaced too far apart, since it was made for adults. But if they stood on tiptoes and reached high above their heads, Frank and Joe could just barely reach the next metal bar above their heads. Slowly they began to pull themselves up.

"Whoa!" Halfway, Frank's hand slipped. For a moment he hung in midair. One hand wasn't enough to hold himself up, though. He could feel his fingers slipping off the smooth, cold metal. He looked down. The ground was a long way away. . . .

"Gotcha!" Joe reached down and grabbed Frank by the wrist. This was the way their dad had taught them. Grabbing someone by the hand made it possible for them to slip out of your grip. But if you grabbed their wrist, the narrowest part of the arm, their hand acted like a stopper and kept them from slipping free. Carefully, Joe pulled Frank back up, until he could grab the bar with both hands.

"Thanks, Joe."

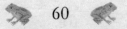

"Don't mention it. Now let's hurry!"

Thankfully, Frank and Joe had a lot of experience climbing things. Their dad had built them a tree house. In there, they wrote up all the cases they had solved, and in the summer they would often climb out onto the high branches.

Finally, they got to the top of the scaffolding. They both scrambled up over the side and found themselves on a small platform.

"Someone could have stood up here and thrown down the frogs," said Joe.

"True," said Frank. He looked around him carefully. "But the floor is made out of metal grating, and anyone who looked up would have seen them. Plus, it would be really hard to carry all the frogs up here!"

The boys looked around. You could see the whole auditorium from up here. They were lucky neither of them was afraid of heights. At least, neither of them was *very* afraid of heights. They both stayed well away from the edge of the platform, just in case.

Then Joe noticed something. "Look! Over there!"

Above the platform, right at one edge, was a broken grate! It was hanging down slightly from the ceiling. It was open just far enough that something the size of a frog could have slipped through it.

"They're everywhere," said Frank. He pointed around the auditorium. Sure enough, it looked like *all* the vents in the ceiling had busted grates—as though a whole lot of something had fallen through them recently.

"That must be how they got in!" said Joe.

"Wherever those grates lead . . . ," said Frank.

"That's where the frogs came from," finished Joe.

"Where do you think they lead?"

"Only one way to find out."

They both looked at the nearest grate. Even standing on tiptoe, there was no way they could reach it alone.

"Here," said Frank. "Get up on my shoulders."

Frank squatted down and held out his hand. Carefully, Joe stepped up, first on Frank's hip, then on his shoulder. Joe used Frank's hand to steady himself. Once he was firmly in place, the front of his shins pressing against the back of Frank's head, Frank stood up. He let go of Joe's hands and held him by the backs of the legs instead, which steadied Joe.

"You okay up there?" Frank asked.

"Yup!" said Joe.

Slowly, Frank made his way over to the edge of the platform.

"I can almost reach it!" said Joe, straining up to catch the edges of the vent beyond the grate.

Frank took another step forward. Now his toes were right up against the edge of the platform.

"Almost—just a little farther."

Frank took a tiny half step. Now his toes were sticking out over the edge, but Joe's weight helped keep him from tipping forward.

"I can't go any farther!" said Frank.

"Got it!" Joe pulled himself up. There were a few seconds of banging, and then Joe's arms reached out from inside the vent.

"Grab my hands," he said.

Frank leaned as far forward as he could, then reached up and grabbed Joe's wrists.

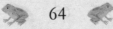

"Ready?" said Frank.

"On the count of three," said Joe.

"One . . . two . . . three!"

On "three," Frank jumped up. Joe pulled as hard as he could. For a second, Frank seemed to hang in the air. Then *zoom!*—up he went into the vent, like a piece of lint being sucked into a vacuum cleaner.

Inside, the vent was dark. There were little patches of light where the grates were, but aside from that, it was a long, dark, narrow tunnel, just wide enough for Frank and Joe to crawl in. Joe began creeping forward, careful not to put any weight on the vents, since they could fall open and send the boys tumbling onto the ground below.

Frank followed Joe, then paused.

"Hey, Joe?"

"Yeah, Frank?"

"How are we going to get back down?"

 65

There was a long pause.

"I hadn't thought about that," said Joe.

After a minute the boys continued crawling. All they could hope for was that the vent would let them out somewhere safe . . . eventually.

In the dark the tunnel got narrower and then wider again. It turned to the left and the right and the left again. It seemed to twist back on itself sometimes. Frank and Joe lost all sense of direction. Once, they came to a ladder and had to climb ten more feet. Eventually, it seemed to get brighter.

"I think there's a way out up ahead!" said Joe. He began to crawl faster. Finally, the boys could make out a square opening at the end of the tunnel. There should have been a grate, like at all the other openings, but this one was missing.

Joe stuck his head out of the hole.

"It's a classroom," he said.

After a few seconds he managed to pull him-

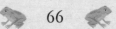

self entirely out of the vent. Frank was right behind him—too close behind him. Frank's arm got tangled up with Joe's leg, and instead of carefully climbing out, the two boys fell out with a loud crash!

*BRAACKSSH!*

They knocked over a desk, and the sound of the metal against the tiled floor was deafening in the quiet room.

Suddenly there was the sound of footsteps approaching. The boys looked up and saw a man in a white lab coat running toward them.

"What are you boys doing?" the man demanded. "Are you with that girl? What did she do with my frogs?"

# 9

# Science to the Rescue!

**M**r. Willis!" said Frank. The man in the lab coat was the fifth-grade science teacher, Mr. Willis. Neither Joe nor Frank had had him as a teacher yet, but Frank knew him from doing extra-credit projects for the science fair.

"Well, my word. Frank Hardy! What are you doing in my classroom?"

"We didn't mean to end up here, sir." Even though he was one of the younger teachers,

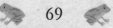 69

Mr. Willis was one of those old-school types who liked to be called "sir" and thought politeness was superimportant.

"Yeah," Joe said, "we were lost in the vents."

Mr. Willis turned to Joe. "And you are . . . ?" he asked.

"Joe. Joe Hardy. Frank's brother."

Mr. Willis continued to stare at him.

"Sir," Joe added. Mr. Willis nodded.

"Well, Joe Hardy. What were you boys doing in

the vents? I'm fairly certain those are not open to the public."

"Well, sir, it's about the talent show . . ."

"The talent show!" Mr. Willis slapped his forehead. "Oh dear. I forgot that was today. And your talent was climbing through the vents?" Mr. Willis had a reputation for being absentminded.

Joe and Frank explained what had happened during the show. While they talked, Mr. Willis straightened up the desk they had knocked over. Finally, after they were done talking, Frank asked him about the girl he had mentioned.

"What girl?" said Mr. Willis.

"The one you mentioned earlier? The girl with the frogs?" said Joe. He was watching the clock at the front of the classroom. Time was running out. In fifteen minutes Principal Butler would call Adam's parents, and then it would all be over.

"Oh yes!" said Mr. Willis. "I was working on an

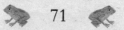

experiment, to try to figure out the different temperatures at which materials burn. I had set up a very interesting array of things. I had four candles and a Bunsen burner prepared. The idea was to take different fabrics, and—"

"Mr. Willis?" Frank interrupted him. "What about the girl?"

"Right!" says Mr. Willis. "Some girl came in because she'd seen the frogs in the aquarium." He pointed to a glass case that sat to the left of the vent the boys had come out of. It was empty.

"She was upset that I was keeping them trapped in here. I explained to her that they had a good life and were safer than they would be in the wild, where predators could get them. Then I turned my back for one minute, and the next thing I know she's gone—and so were my frogs!"

"They must be the frogs that ended up falling on the talent show," said Joe.

"I knew Adam didn't do it!" said Frank.

"Oh dear! I hope the frogs weren't injured. Do you know where they are now? I need them for class tomorrow," said Mr. Willis.

"Principal Butler has them in her office, I think."

"That is great news! I'm going to go get them now."

PLEASE HANDLE
THE FROGS
CAREFULLY...
...MR. WILLIS

Mr. Willis turned away from Frank and Joe. He nearly ran out of the room.

"Wait!" yelled Joe. "The girl—who was it?"

"She didn't introduce herself, I'm afraid."

"What did she look like, sir?" asked Joe.

"Well . . . she was short. And had hair. You know. Like a girl."

That wasn't going to be enough to go on. Joe tried again. "Was there anything different about her? Anything that would help you find her again?"

Mr. Willis thought for a moment. He pulled his long hair distractedly.

"Oh yes! She was dressed funny—like a bumblebee. Now I really must go find my frogs. Good-bye, boys!"

Mr. Willis ran out of the room.

"Dressed like a bumblebee?" said Frank. "Who could that be? Was anyone wearing wings for the talent show?"

"No," said Joe. "But Melissa was dressed in yellow and black! And she said she loves frogs."

Was Melissa responsible for ruining her own number?

# 10

# The Show Must Go On

"Excuse me! Sorry! Coming through!"

Frank and Joe ran through the halls of Bayport Elementary as fast as they could go. They had to talk to Melissa before Principal Butler got out of her meeting. When they got to the door to the auditorium, they could hear singing coming from inside. They were in luck! Melissa was still rehearsing.

They burst through the doors. Melissa and Todd stopped singing. Before they could say anything, Frank burst out with, "Did you take the frogs from Mr. Willis's classroom?"

Melissa looked stunned. "No! I didn't . . . *take* them."

Something about the way she said it told Frank she was lying.

"Did you touch them?"

"It wasn't my fault! They were being kept imprisoned! I was going to take them outside, but then Mr. Willis came running in and yelled at me, and I turned around to grab them off the counter where I had put them, and they were gone!" Melissa had started crying. This time, Frank believed her.

"They must have hopped off the counter, into the open vent!" said Joe.

"I just wanted them to be free!" said Melissa.

"You're going to have to tell Principal Butler," said Frank.

"But I didn't bring them to the talent show. Adam said he did it!" Melissa didn't want to get in trouble.

Frank and Joe explained their theory: The frogs had escaped into the system of vents. When they reached the auditorium, they had broken the grates and fallen through.

"Oh no!" said Melissa. "It *is* all my fault."

Together, Melissa, Todd, Frank, and Joe headed to Principal Butler's office. When they arrived, Principal Butler was just about to call Adam's parents. Adam and Mina were sitting in the office with her.

Melissa, Frank, and Joe explained what had happened.

"I'm sorry, Principal Butler! I just love frogs so much," Melissa cried.

Principal Butler pushed her glasses up the bridge of her nose and thought for a second.

 78

"I believe you, Melissa. Since this was an accident, and the only performance you ruined was your own, I'm not going to call your parents. Instead, you will be volunteering with Mr. Willis for the rest of the school year. Your job will be to take care of the frogs."

"Really? Oh, wow!" Melissa said. Frank and Joe had never seen her this excited—even when her Tasty, Tasty Treats Ice Cream commercial was aired for the first time!

"As for you, Mr. Ackerman, you will explain yourself right now."

Adam looked down at his shoes and said nothing. Mina jumped in.

"He just didn't want anyone to know that he couldn't have thrown the frogs, because he was singing to me! I got so scared to perform, I hid in the janitor's closet. Adam came and sang to me, like he used to when I was little and scared of the dark."

 79

Even Principal Butler smiled at what Mina had to say. It seemed no one believed Adam's denial. The big, bad bully, singing to his sister? No wonder he would rather have confessed to a crime he didn't commit!

"That's not true!" Adam yelled. "I don't sing! Never! And if you tell anyone, I'm totally going to get you!"

Adam stomped out of Principal Butler's office. Principal Butler stood up from behind her desk.

"Well, now that all of that is cleared up, let's get the talent show back on!"

"Yay!" Everyone cheered.

The rest of the talent show went smoothly. Melissa and Todd got to perform their number— without any frogs this time. They were great, as usual. Then the boys were up. With all of the crime solving, they'd almost forgotten they were going to perform! Everyone loved their sword fighting, and they got a big round of applause when they finished. There were a few more acts after them, and then finally, it was time to vote.

Everyone was given a little slip of paper with all the acts listed. It was hard to vote for just one, but both Frank and Joe knew who their favorite was— Cissy! It would be wrong to vote for themselves, and Cissy deserved it the most. Her juggling was so incredible.

It seemed like Frank and Joe weren't the only ones who loved Cissy's act. When the votes were counted, she was in first place!

"Wow!" she screamed. This was the first time in years that anyone other than Melissa and Todd had gotten first place. Cissy couldn't stop thanking everyone all the way to the winner's platform. "This is amazing. I mean, I never expected to win. Thank you all so much! Thank you, thank you, thank you."

Melissa and Todd came in second. Melissa was so excited about getting to take care of the frogs that she didn't even seem upset that she hadn't won first place. Then Principal Butler read off the third-place winner.

"In third place, Frank and Joe Hardy!"

Third place? Wow! Who would have guessed? Today was the best day ever!

• • • •

After all the excitement of the day, Frank and Joe were happy to get back to their tree house. On their big blackboard, they wrote *Secret Files Case #4: Solved!* They were just about to pin their winner's ribbon up on the wall when someone crawled up the ladder and into the tree house with them.

"Hey, Frank! Hey, Joe! How's it going?"

"Hey, Cissy! What's up?" Cissy was one of the few people the boys allowed up in their tree house at any time.

"I just had to give this to you," Cissy said, holding out the first-place ribbon. "If it wasn't for the two of you, and your other special talent, none of us would have won today. The whole show would have been canceled. You guys really deserve first place!"

"No way!" said Frank. He shook his head. Cissy deserved that ribbon.

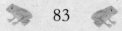

"Your juggling act was amazing!" said Joe.

But Cissy insisted they take first place. Finally, Frank had an idea.

"How about we share first place?"

Cissy thought for a moment.

"Deal!" she said.